RAM NAM SATH

AKHIL

this book is ....

Contents

ONE

SEVERAL NEW INPUT

From 1983 onward, several new input techniques were developed and included in laptops, including the touch pad (Gavilan SC, 1983), the pointing stick (IBM ThinkPad 700, 1992), and handwriting recognition (Linus Write-Top,[23] 1987). Some CPUs, such as the 1990 Intel i386SL, were designed to use minimum power to increase battery life of portable computers and were supported by dynamic power management features such as Intel SpeedStep and AMD PowerNow! in some designs.

Displays reached 640x480 (VGA) resolution by 1988 (Compaq SLT/286), and color screens started becoming a common upgrade in 1991,[24] with increases in resolution and screen size occurring frequently until the introduction of 17" screen laptops in 2003. Hard drives started to be used in portables, encouraged by the introduction of 3.5" drives in the late 1980s, and became common in laptops starting with the introduction of 2.5" and smaller drives around 1990; capacities have typically lagged behind physically larger desktop drives.

Common resolutions of laptop webcams are 720p (HD), and in lower-end laptops 480p.[25] The earliest known laptops with 1080p (Full HD) webcams like the Samsung 700G7C were released in the early 2010s.[26]

Optical disc drives became common in full-size laptops around 1997; this initially consisted of CD-ROM drives, which were supplanted by CD-R, DVD, and Blu-ray drives with writing capability over time. Starting around 2011, the trend shifted against internal optical drives, and as of 2021, they have largely disappeared; they are still readily available as external peripherals.

Etymology[edit]

While the terms laptop and notebook are used interchangeably today, there is some question as to the original etymology and specificity of either term. The term laptop appears to have been coined in the early 1980s to describe a mobile computer which could be used on one's lap and to distinguish these devices from earlier and much heavier portable computers (informally called "luggables"). The term notebook appears to have gained currency somewhat later as manufacturers started producing even smaller portable devices, further reducing their weight and size and incorporating a display roughly the size of A4 paper;[3] these were marketed as notebooks to distinguish them from bulkier mainstream or desktop replacement laptops.

Types[edit]

Compaq Armada laptop from the late 1990s

Apple MacBook Air, an "ultraportable" laptop weighing under 3.0 lb (1.36 kg)

Lenovo's IdeaPad laptop

Lenovo's ThinkPad business laptop, originally an IBM product

Acer Aspire laptop

Asus Transformer Pad, a hybrid tablet, powered by Android OS

Microsoft Surface Pro 3, 2-in-1 detachable

Alienware gaming laptop with backlit keyboard and touch pad

Samsung Sens laptop

Samsung Notebook 3

Panasonic Toughbook CF-M34, a rugged laptop/subnotebook

Since the introduction of portable computers during the late 1970s, their form has changed significantly, spawning a variety of visually and technologically differing subclasses. Except where there is a distinct legal trademark around a term (notably, Ultrabook), there are rarely hard distinctions between these classes and their usage has varied over time and between different sources. Since the late 2010s, the use of more specific terms has become less common, with sizes distinguished largely by the size of the screen.

Smaller and Larger Laptops[edit]

Main articles: Subnotebook and Desktop replacement computer

There were in the past a number of marketing categories for smaller and larger laptop computers; these included "subnotebook" models, low cost "netbooks", and "Ultra-mobile PCs" where the size class overlapped with devices like smartphone and handheld tablets, and "Desktop replacement" laptops for machines notably larger and heavier than typical to operate more powerful processors or graphics hardware.[27] All of these terms have fallen out of favor as the size of mainstream laptops has gone down and their capabilities have gone up; except for niche models, laptop sizes tend to be distinguished by the size of the screen, and for more powerful models, by any specialized purpose the machine is intended for, such as a "gaming laptop" or a "mobile workstation" for professional use.

See also: Gaming computer § Gaming laptop computers, and Workstation

Convertible, hybrid, 2-in-1[edit]

This section does not cite any sources. Please help improve this section by adding citations to reliable sources. Unsourced material may be challenged and removed. (November 2015) (Learn how and when to remove this template message)

Main article: 2-in-1 PC

The latest trend of technological convergence in the portable computer industry spawned a broad range of devices, which combined features of several previously separate device types. The hybrids, convertibles, and 2-in-1s emerged as crossover devices, which share traits of both tablets and laptops. All such devices have a touchscreen display designed to allow users to work in a tablet mode, using either multi-touch gestures or a stylus/digital pen.

Convertibles are devices with the ability to conceal a hardware keyboard. Keyboards on such devices can be flipped, rotated, or slid behind the back of the chassis, thus transforming from a laptop into a tablet. Hybrids have a keyboard detachment mechanism, and due to this feature, all critical components are situated in the part with the display. 2-in-1s can have a hybrid or a convertible form, often dubbed 2-in-1 detachable and 2-in-1 convertibles respectively, but are distinguished by the ability to run a desktop OS, such as Windows 10. 2-in-1s are often marketed as laptop replacement tablets.[28]

2-in-1s are often very thin, around 10 millimetres (0.39 in), and light devices with a long battery life. 2-in-1s are distinguished from mainstream tablets as they feature an x86-architecture CPU (typically a low- or ultra-low-voltage model), such as the Intel Core i5, run a full-featured desktop OS like Windows 10, and have a number of typical laptop I/O ports, such as USB 3 and Mini DisplayPort.

2-in-1s are designed to be used not only as a media consumption device but also as valid desktop or laptop replacements, due to their ability to run desktop applications, such as Adobe Photoshop. It is possible to connect multiple peripheral devices, such as a mouse, keyboard, and several external displays to a modern 2-in-1.

Microsoft Surface Pro-series devices and Surface Book are examples of modern 2-in-1 detachable, whereas Lenovo Yoga-series computers are a variant of 2-in-1 convertibles. While the older Surface RT and Surface 2 have the same chassis design as the Surface Pro, their use of ARM processors and Windows RT do not classify them as 2-in-1s, but as hybrid tablets.[29] Similarly, a number of hybrid laptops run a mobile operating system, such as Android. These include Asus's Transformer Pad devices, examples of hybrids with a detachable keyboard design, which do not fall in the category of 2-in-1s.

Rugged laptop[edit]

Main article: Rugged computer

A rugged laptop is designed to reliably operate in harsh usage conditions such as strong vibrations, extreme temperatures, and wet or dusty environments. Rugged laptops are bulkier, heavier, and much more expensive than regular laptops,[30] and thus are seldom seen in regular consumer use.

Hardware[edit]

This section needs additional citations for verification. Please help improve this article by adding citations to reliable sources. Unsourced material may be challenged and removed. (July 2016) (Learn how and when to remove this template message)

Main article: Personal computer hardware

Miniaturization: a comparison of a desktop computer motherboard (ATX form factor) to a motherboard from a 13" laptop (2008 unibody MacBook)

Inner view of a Sony VAIO laptop

A SODIMM memory module

The basic components of laptops function identically to their desktop counterparts. Traditionally they were miniaturized and adapted to mobile use, although desktop systems increasingly use the same smaller, lower-power parts which were originally developed for mobile use. The design restrictions on power, size, and cooling of laptops limit the maximum performance of laptop parts compared to that of desktop components, although that difference has increasingly narrowed.[31]

In general, laptop components are not intended to be replaceable or upgradable by the end-user, except for components that can be detached; in the past, batteries and optical drives were commonly exchangeable. This restriction is one of the major differences between laptops and desktop computers, because the large "tower" cases used in desktop computers are designed so that new motherboards, hard disks, sound cards, RAM, and other components can be added. Memory and storage can often be upgraded with some disassembly, but with the most compact laptops, there may be no upgradeable components at all.[32]

Intel, Asus, Compal, Quanta, and some other laptop manufacturers have created the Common Building Block standard for laptop parts to address some of the inefficiencies caused by the lack of standards and inability to upgrade components.[33]

The following sections summarizes the differences and distinguishing features of laptop components in comparison to desktop personal computer parts.[34]

Display[edit]

Internally, a display is usually an LCD panel, although occasionally OLEDs are used. These interface to the laptop using the LVDS or embedded DisplayPort protocol, while externally, it can be a glossy screen or a matte (anti-glare) screen. As of 2021, mainstream consumer laptops tend to come with either 13" or 15"-16" screens; 14" models are more popular among business machines. Larger and smaller models are available, but less common – there is no clear dividing line in minimum or maximum size. Machines small enough to be handheld (screens in the 6–8" range) can be marketed either as very small laptops or "handheld PCs," while the distinction between the largest laptops and "All-in-One" desktops is whether they fold for travel.

Sizes[edit]

In the past, there was a broader range of marketing terms (both formal and informal) to distinguish between different sizes of laptops. These included Netbooks, subnotebooks, Ultra-mobile PC, and Desktop replacement computers; these are sometimes still used informally, although they are essentially dead in terms of manufacturer marketing.

Resolution[edit]

Having a higher resolution display allows more items to fit onscreen at a time, improving the user's ability to multitask, although at the higher resolutions on smaller screens, the resolution may only serve to display sharper graphics and text rather than increasing the usable area.

Since the introduction of the MacBook Pro with Retina display in 2012, there have been an increase in the availability of "HiDPI" (or high Pixel density) displays; as of 2021, this is generally considered to be anything higher than 1920 pixels wide. This has increasingly converged around 4K (3840-pixel-wide) resolutions.

External displays can be connected to most laptops, and models with a Mini DisplayPort can handle up to three.[35]

Refresh rates and 3D[edit]

The earliest laptops known to feature a display with doubled 120 Hz of refresh rate and active shutter 3D system were released in 2011 by Dell (M17x) and Samsung (700G7A).[36][37]

Central processing unit[edit]

A laptop's central processing unit (CPU) has advanced power-saving features and produces less heat than one intended purely for desktop use. Mainstream laptop CPUs made after 2018 have four processor cores, although some inexpensive models still have 2-core CPUs, and 6-core and 8-core models are also available.

For the low price and mainstream performance, there is no longer a significant performance difference between laptop and desktop CPUs, but at the high end, the fastest desktop CPUs still substantially outperform the fastest laptop processors, at the expense of massively higher power consumption and heat generation; the fastest laptop processors top out at 56 watts of heat, while the fastest desktop processors top out at 150 watts.

There has been a wide range of CPUs designed for laptops available from both Intel, AMD, and other manufacturers. On non-x86 architectures, Motorola and IBM produced the chips for the former PowerPC-based Apple laptops (iBook and PowerBook). Between around

2000 to 2014, most full-size laptops had socketed, replaceable CPUs; on thinner models, the CPU was soldered on the motherboard and was not replaceable or upgradable without replacing the motherboard. Since 2015, Intel has not offered new laptop CPU models with pins to be interchangeable, preferring ball grid array chip packages which have to be soldered;[38]and as of 2021, only a few rare models using desktop parts.

In the past, some laptops have used a desktop processor instead of the laptop version and have had high-performance gains at the cost of greater weight, heat, and limited battery life; this is not unknown as of 2021, but since around 2010, the practice has been restricted to small-volume gaming models. Laptop CPUs are rarely able to be overclocked; most use locked processors. Even on gaming models where unlocked processors are available, the cooling system in most laptops is often very close to its limits and there is rarely headroom for an overclocking–related operating temperature increase.

Graphical processing unit[edit]

On most laptops, a graphical processing unit (GPU) is integrated into the CPU to conserve power and space. This was introduced by Intel with the Core i-series of mobile processors in 2010, and similar accelerated processing unit (APU) processors by AMD later that year.

Before that, lower-end machines tended to use graphics processors integrated into the system chipset, while higher-end machines had a separate graphics processor. In the past, laptops lacking a separate graphics processor were limited in their utility for gaming and professional applications involving 3D graphics, but the capabilities of CPU-integrated graphics have converged with the low-end of dedicated graphics processors since the mid-2010s.

Higher-end laptops intended for gaming or professional 3D work still come with dedicated and in some cases even dual, graphics processors on the motherboard or as an internal expansion card. Since 2011, these almost always involve switchable graphics so that when there is no demand for the higher performance dedicated graphics processor, the more power-efficient integrated graphics processor will be used. Nvidia Optimus and AMD Hybrid Graphics are examples of this sort of system of switchable graphics.

Memory[edit]

Since around the year 2000, most laptops have used SO-DIMM RAM,[34] although, as of 2021, an increasing number of models use memory soldered to the motherboard. Before 2000, most laptops used proprietary memory modules if their memory was upgradable.

In the early 2010s, high end laptops such as the 2011 Samsung 700G7A have passed the 10 GB RAM barrier, featuring 16 GB of RAM.[39]

When upgradeable, memory slots are sometimes accessible from the bottom of the laptop for ease of upgrading; in other cases, accessing them requires significant disassembly. Most laptops have two memory slots, although some will have only one, either for cost savings or because some amount of memory is soldered. Some high-end models have four slots; these are usually mobile engineering workstations, although a few high-end models intended for gaming do as well.

As of 2021, 8 GB RAM is most common, with lower-end models occasionally having 4GB. Higher-end laptops may come with 16 GB of RAM or more.

Internal storage[edit]

The earliest laptops most often used floppy disk for storage, although a few used either RAM disks or tape, by the late 1980s hard disk drives had become the standard form of storage.

Between 1990 and 2009, almost all laptops typically had a hard disk drive (HDD) for storage; since then, solid-state drives (SSD) have gradually come to supplant hard drives in all but some inexpensive consumer models. Solid-state drives are faster and more power-efficient, as well as eliminating the hazard of drive and data corruption caused by a laptop's physical impacts, as they use no mechanical parts such as a rotational platter.[40] In many cases, they are more compact as well. Initially, in the late 2000s, SSDs were substantially more expensive than HDDs, but as of 2021 prices on smaller capacity (under 1 terabyte) drives have converged; larger capacity drives remain more expensive than comparable-sized HDDs.

Since around 1990, where a hard drive is present it will typically be a 2.5-inch drive; some very compact laptops support even smaller 1.8-inch HDDs, and a very small number used 1" Microdrives. Some SSDs are built to match the size/shape of a laptop hard drive, but increasingly they have been replaced with smaller mSATA or M.2 cards. SSDs using the newer and much faster NVM Express standard for connecting are only available as cards.

As of 2021, many laptops no longer contain space for a 2.5" drive, accepting only M.2 cards; a few of the smallest have storage soldered to the motherboard. For those that can, they can typically contain a single 2.5-inch drive, but a small number of laptops with a screen wider than 15 inches can house two drives.

A variety of external HDDs or NAS data storage servers with support of RAID technology can be attached to virtually any laptop over such interfaces as USB, FireWire, eSATA, or Thunderbolt, or over a wired or wireless network to further increase space for the storage of data. Many laptops also incorporate a card reader which allows for use of memory cards, such as those used for digital cameras, which are typically SD or microSD cards. This enables users to download digital pictures from an SD card onto a laptop, thus enabling them to delete the SD card's contents to free up space for taking new pictures.

Removable media drive[edit]

Optical disc drives capable of playing CD-ROMs, compact discs (CD), DVDs, and in some cases, Blu-ray discs (BD), were nearly universal on full-sized models between the mid-1990s and the early 2010s. As of 2021, drives are uncommon in compact or premium laptops; they remain available in some bulkier models, but the trend towards thinner and lighter machines is gradually eliminating these drives and players – when needed they can be connected via USB instead.

Inputs[edit]

Closeup of a touchpad on an Acer laptop, where buttons and the touch-sensitive surface are shared

Closeup of a TrackPoint cursor and UltraNav buttons on a ThinkPad laptop

Interfaces on a ThinkPad laptop (2011): Ethernet network port (center), VGA (left), DisplayPort (top right) and USB 2.0 (bottom right). Due to the trend towards very flat laptops and the widespread use of WLAN, the relatively high Ethernet socket is no longer mandatory in today's devices, as is the technically outdated VGA.

An alphanumeric keyboard is used to enter text, data, and other commands (e.g., function keys). A touchpad (also called a trackpad), a pointing stick, or both, are used to control the position of the cursor on the screen, and an integrated keyboard[41] is used for typing. Some touchpads have buttons separate from the touch surface, while others share the surface. A quick double-tap is typically registered as a click, and operating systems may recognize multi-finger touch gestures.

An external keyboard and mouse may be connected using a USB port or wirelessly, via Bluetooth or similar technology. Some laptops have multitouch touchscreen displays, either available as an option or standard. Most laptops have webcams and microphones, which can be used to communicate with other people with both moving images and sound, via web conferencing or video-calling software.

Laptops typically have USB ports and a combined headphone/microphone jack, for use with headphones, a combined headset, or an external mic. Many laptops have a card reader for reading digital camera SD cards.

Input/output (I/O) ports[edit]

On a typical laptop there are several USB ports; if they use only the older USB connectors instead of USB-C, they will typically have an external monitor port (VGA, DVI, HDMI or Mini DisplayPort or occasionally more than one), an audio in/out port (often in form of a single socket) is common. It is possible to connect up to three external displays to a 2014-era laptop via a single Mini DisplayPort, using multi-stream transport technology.[35]

Apple, in a 2015 version of its MacBook, transitioned from a number of different I/O ports to a single USB-C port.[42] This port can be used both for charging and connecting a variety of devices through the use of aftermarket adapters. Google, with its updated version of Chromebook Pixel, shows a similar transition trend towards USB-C, although keeping older USB Type-A ports for a better compatibility with older devices.[43] Although being common until the end of the 2000s decade, Ethernet network port are rarely found on modern laptops, due to widespread use of wireless networking, such as Wi-Fi. Legacy ports such as a PS/2 keyboard/mouse port, serial port, parallel port, or FireWire are provided on some models, but they are increasingly rare. On Apple's systems, and on a handful of other laptops, there are also Thunderbolt ports, but Thunderbolt 3 uses USB-C. Laptops typically have a headphone jack, so that the user can connect external headphones or amplified speaker systems for listening to music or other audio.

Expansion cards[edit]

In the past, a PC Card (formerly PCMCIA) or ExpressCard slot for expansion was often present on laptops to allow adding and removing functionality, even when the laptop is powered on; these are becoming increasingly rare since the introduction of USB 3.0. Some internal subsystems such as Ethernet, Wi-Fi, or a wireless cellular modem can be implemented as replaceable internal expansion cards, usually accessible under an access cover on the bottom of the laptop. The standard for such cards is PCI Express, which comes in both mini and even smaller M.2 sizes. In newer laptops, it is not uncommon to also see Micro SATA (mSATA) functionality on PCI Express Mini or M.2 card slots allowing the use of those slots for SATA-based solid-state drives.[44]

Battery and power supply[edit]

Main article: Smart battery

Almost all laptops use smart batteries

Since the late 1990s, laptops have typically used lithium ion or lithium polymer batteries, These replaced the older nickel metal-hydride typically used in the 1990s, and nickel–cadmium batteries used in most of the earliest laptops. A few of the oldest laptops used non-rechargeable batteries, or lead–acid batteries.

Battery life is highly variable by model and workload and can range from one hour to nearly a day. A battery's performance gradually decreases over time; a substantial reduction in capacity is typically evident after one to three years of regular use, depending on the charging and discharging pattern and the design of the battery. Innovations in laptops and batteries have seen situations in which the battery can provide up to 24 hours of continued operation, assuming average power consumption levels. An example is the HP EliteBook 6930p when used with its ultra-capacity battery.[45]

A 2011 laptop with extended capacity replacement battery inserted.

Laptops with removable batteries may support larger replacement batteries with extended capacity.

A laptop's battery is charged using an external power supply, which is plugged into a wall outlet. The power supply outputs a DC voltage typically in the range of 7.2—24 volts. The power supply is usually external and connected to the laptop through a DC connector cable. In most cases, it can charge the battery and power the laptop simultaneously. When the battery is fully charged, the laptop continues to run on power supplied by the external power supply, avoiding battery use. If the used power supply is not strong enough to power computing components and charge the battery simultaneously, the battery may charge in a shorter period of time if the laptop is turned off or sleeping. The charger typically adds about 400 grams (0.88 lb) to the overall transporting weight of a laptop, although some models are substantially heavier or lighter. Most 2016-era laptops use a smart battery, a rechargeable battery pack with a built-in battery management system (BMS). The smart battery can internally measure voltage and current, and deduce charge level and State of Health (SoH) parameters, indicating the state of the cells.[citation needed]

Power connectors[edit]

Laptop power supply with cylindrical coaxial DC power connector

Historically, DC connectors, typically cylindrical/barrel-shaped coaxial power connectors have been used in laptops. Some vendors such as Lenovo made intermittent use of a rectangular connector.

Some connector heads feature a center pin to allow the end device to determine the power supply type by measuring the resistance between it and the connector's negative pole (outer surface). Vendors may block charging if a power supply is not recognized as original part, which could deny the legitimate use of universal third-party chargers.[46]

USB-C connector

With the advent of USB-C, portable electronics made increasing use of it for both power delivery and data transfer. Its support for 20 V (common laptop power supply voltage) and 5 A typically suffices for low to mid-end laptops, but some with higher power demands such as gaming laptops depend on dedicated DC connectors to handle currents beyond 5 A without risking overheating, some even above 10 A. Additionally, dedicated DC connectors are more durable and less prone to wear and tear from frequent reconnection, as their design is less delicate.[47]

Cooling[edit]

Waste heat from the operation is difficult to remove in the compact internal space of a laptop. The earliest laptops used passive cooling; this gave way to heat sinks placed directly on the components to be cooled, but when these hot components are deep inside the device, a large space-wasting air duct is needed to exhaust the heat. Modern laptops instead rely on heat pipes to rapidly move waste heat towards the edges of the device, to allow for a much smaller and compact fan and heat sink cooling system. Waste heat is usually exhausted away from the device operator towards the rear or sides of the device. Multiple air intake paths are used since some intakes can be blocked, such as when the device is placed on a soft conforming surface like a chair cushion. Secondary device temperature monitoring may reduce performance or trigger an emergency shutdown if it is unable to dissipate heat, such as if the laptop were to be left running and placed inside a carrying case. Aftermarket cooling pads with external fans can be used with laptops to reduce operating temperatures.

Docking station[edit]

Docking station and laptop

A docking station (sometimes referred to simply as a dock) is a laptop accessory that contains multiple ports and in some cases expansion slots or bays for fixed or removable drives. A laptop connects and disconnects to a docking station, typically through a single large proprietary connector. A docking station is an especially popular laptop accessory in a corporate computing environment, due to a possibility of a docking station transforming a laptop into a full-featured desktop replacement, yet allowing for its easy release. This ability can be advantageous to "road warrior" employees who have to travel frequently for work, and yet who also come into the office. If more ports are needed, or their position on a laptop is inconvenient, one can use a cheaper passive device known as a port replicator. These devices mate to the connectors on the laptop, such as through USB or FireWire.

Charging trolleys[edit]

Laptop charging trolleys, also known as laptop trolleys or laptop carts, are mobile storage containers to charge multiple laptops, netbooks, and tablet computers at the same time. The trolleys are used in schools that have replaced their traditional static computer labs[48] suites of desktop equipped with "tower" computers, but do not have enough plug sockets in an individual classroom to charge all of the devices. The trolleys can be wheeled between rooms and classrooms so that all students and teachers in a particular building can access fully charged IT equipment.[49]

Laptop charging trolleys are also used to deter and protect against opportunistic and organized theft. Schools, especially those with open plan designs, are often prime targets for thieves who steal high-value items. Laptops, netbooks, and tablets are among the highest–value portable items in a school. Moreover, laptops can easily be concealed under clothing and stolen from buildings. Many types of laptop–charging trolleys are designed and constructed to protect against theft. They are generally made out of steel, and the laptops remain locked up while not in use. Although the trolleys can be moved between areas from one classroom to another, they can often be mounted or locked to the floor, support pillars, or walls to prevent thieves from stealing the laptops, especially overnight.[48]

Solar panels[edit]

Main article: Solar notebook

In some laptops, solar panels are able to generate enough solar power for the laptop to operate.[50] The One Laptop Per Child Initiative released the OLPC XO-1 laptop which was tested and successfully operated by use of solar panels.[51] Presently, they are designing an OLPC XO-3 laptop with these features. The OLPC XO-3 can operate with 2 watts of electricity because its renewable energy resources generate a total of 4 watts.[52][53] Samsung has also designed the NC215S solar–powered notebook that will be sold commercially in the U.S. market.[54]

Accessories[edit]

A common accessory for laptops is a laptop sleeve, laptop skin, or laptop case, which provides a degree of protection from scratches. Sleeves, which are distinguished by being relatively thin and flexible, are most commonly made of neoprene, with sturdier ones made of low-resilience polyurethane. Some laptop sleeves are wrapped in ballistic nylon to provide some measure of waterproofing. Bulkier and sturdier cases can be made of metal with polyurethane padding inside and may have locks for added security. Metal, padded cases also offer protection against impacts and drops. Another common accessory is a laptop cooler, a device that helps lower the internal temperature of the laptop either actively or passively. A common active method involves using electric fans to draw heat away from the laptop, while a passive method might involve propping the laptop up on some type of pad so it can receive more airflow. Some stores sell laptop pads that enable a reclining person on a bed to use a laptop.

Modularity[edit]

Opened bottom covers allow replacement of RAM and storage modules (Lenovo G555)

Some of the components of earlier models of laptops can easily be replaced without opening completely its bottom part, such as keyboard, battery, hard disk, memory modules, CPU cooling fan, etc.

Some of the components of recent models of laptops reside inside. Replacing most of its components, such as keyboard, battery, hard disk, memory modules, CPU cooling fan, etc., requires removal of its either top or bottom part, removal of the motherboard, and returning them.

In some types, solder and glue are used to mount components such as RAM, storage, and batteries, making repairs additionally difficult.[55][56]

Obsolete features[edit]

A modem PCMCIA card on an old ThinkPad. The card would normally fully insert into the socket.

Features that certain early models of laptops used to have that are not available in most current laptops include:

Reset ("cold restart") button in a hole (needed a thin metal tool to press)

Instant power off button in a hole (needed a thin metal tool to press)

Integrated charger or power adapter inside the laptop

Floppy disk drive

Serial port

Parallel port

Modem

Shared PS/2 input device port

IrDA

S-video port[note 1]

S/PDIF audio port

PC Card / PCMCIA slot

ExpressCard slot

CD/DVD Drives (starting with 2013 models)

VGA port (starting with 2013 models)

Comparison with desktops[edit]

Advantages[edit]

A teacher using the laptop as part of a workshop for school children

Wikipedia co-founder Jimmy Wales using a laptop on a park bench

Portability is usually the first feature mentioned in any comparison of laptops versus desktop PCs.[57] Physical portability allows a laptop to be used in many places—not only at home and the office but also during commuting and flights, in coffee shops, in lecture halls and libraries, at clients' locations or a meeting room, etc. Within a home, portability enables laptop users to move their devices from the living room to the dining room to the family room. Portability offers several distinct advantages:

Productivity: Using a laptop in places where a desktop PC cannot be used can help employees and students to increase their productivity on work or school tasks, such as an office worker reading their work e-mails during an hour-long commute by train, or a student doing their homework at the university coffee shop during a break between lectures, for example.

Immediacy: Carrying a laptop means having instant access to information, including personal and work files. This allows better collaboration between coworkers or students, as a laptop can be flipped open to look at a report, document, spreadsheet, or presentation anytime and anywhere.

Up-to-date information: If a person has more than one desktop PC, a problem of synchronization arises: changes made on one computer are not automatically propagated to the others. There are ways to resolve this problem, including physical transfer of updated files (using a USB flash memory stick or CD-ROMs) or using synchronization software over the Internet, such as cloud computing. However, transporting a single laptop to both locations avoids the problem entirely, as the files exist in a single location and are always up-to-date.

Connectivity: In the 2010s, a proliferation of Wi-Fi wireless networks and cellular broadband data services (HSDPA, EVDO and others) in many urban centers, combined with near-ubiquitous Wi-Fi support by modern laptops[note 2] meant that a laptop could now have easy Internet and local network connectivity while remaining mobile. Wi-Fi networks and laptop programs are especially widespread at university campuses.[58]

Other advantages of laptops:

Size: Laptops are smaller than desktop PCs. This is beneficial when space is at a premium, for example in small apartments and student dorms. When not in use, a laptop can be closed and put away in a desk drawer.

Low power consumption: Laptops are several times more power-efficient than desktops. A typical laptop uses 20–120 W, compared to 100–800 W for desktops. This could be particularly beneficial for large businesses, which run hundreds of personal computers thus multiplying the potential savings, and homes where there is a computer running 24/7 (such as a home media server, print server, etc.).

Quiet: Laptops are typically much quieter than desktops, due both to the components (quieter, slower 2.5-inch hard drives) and to less heat production leading to the use of fewer and slower cooling fans.

Battery: a charged laptop can continue to be used in case of a power outage and is not affected by short power interruptions and blackouts. A desktop PC needs an uninterruptible power supply (UPS) to handle short interruptions, blackouts, and spikes; achieving on-battery time of more than 20–30 minutes for a desktop PC requires a large and expensive UPS.[59]

All-in-One: designed to be portable, most 2010-era laptops have all components integrated into the chassis (however, some small laptops may not have an internal CD/CDR/DVD drive, so an external drive needs to be used). For desktops (excluding all-in-ones) this is usually divided into the desktop "tower" (the unit with the CPU, hard drive, power supply, etc.), keyboard, mouse, display screen, and optional peripherals such as speakers.

Disadvantages[edit]

Compared to desktop PCs, laptops have disadvantages in the following areas:

Performance[edit]

Parts of this article (those related to sub-section) need to be updated. The reason given is: info is since 2008, nearly 13 years old. Please help update this article to reflect recent events or newly available information. (April 2021)

While the performance of mainstream desktops and laptops are comparable, and the cost of laptops has fallen less rapidly than desktops, laptops remain more expensive than desktop PCs at the same performance level.[60][needs update] The upper limits of performance of laptops remain much lower than the highest-end desktops (especially "workstation class" machines with two processor sockets), and "leading-edge" features usually appear first in desktops and only then, as the underlying technology matures, are adapted to laptops.

For Internet browsing and typical office applications, where the computer spends the majority of its time waiting for the next user input, even relatively low-end laptops (such as Netbooks) can be fast enough for some users.[61] Most higher-end laptops are sufficiently powerful for high-resolution movie playback, some 3D gaming and video editing and encoding. However, laptop processors can be disadvantaged when dealing with a higher-end database, maths, engineering, financial software, virtualization, etc. This is because laptops use the mobile versions of processors to conserve power, and these lag behind desktop chips when it comes to performance. Some manufacturers work around this performance problem by using desktop CPUs for laptops.[62]

Upgradeability[edit]

The upgradeability of laptops is very limited compared to thoroughly standardized desktops. In general, hard drives and memory can be upgraded easily. Optical drives and internal expansion cards may be upgraded if they follow an industry standard, but all other internal components, including the motherboard, CPU, and graphics, are not always intended to be upgradeable. Intel, Asus, Compal, Quanta and some other laptop manufacturers have created the Common Building Block standard for laptop parts to address some of the inefficiencies caused by the lack of standards. The reasons for limited upgradeability are both technical and economic. There is no industry-wide standard form factor for laptops; each major laptop manufacturer pursues its own proprietary design and construction, with the result that laptops are difficult to upgrade and have high repair costs. Moreover, starting with 2013 models, laptops have become increasingly integrated (soldered) with the motherboard for most of its components (CPU, SSD, RAM, keyboard, etc.) to reduce size and upgradeability prospects. Devices such as sound cards, network adapters, hard and optical drives, and numerous other peripherals are available, but these upgrades usually impair the laptop's portability, because they add cables and boxes to the setup and often have to be disconnected and reconnected when the laptop is on the move.[citation needed]

Ergonomics and health effects[edit]

Wrists[edit]

Laptop cooler (silver) under laptop (white), preventing heating of lap and improving laptop airflow

Prolonged use of laptops can cause repetitive strain injury because of their small, flat keyboard and trackpad pointing devices.[63] Usage of separate, external ergonomic keyboards and pointing devices is recommended to prevent injury when working for long periods of time; they can be connected to a laptop easily by USB, Bluetooth or via a docking station. Some health standards require ergonomic keyboards at workplaces.

Neck and spine[edit]

A laptop's integrated screen often requires users to lean over for a better view, which can cause neck or spinal injuries. A larger and higher-quality external screen can be connected to almost any laptop to alleviate this and to provide additional screen space for more productive work. Another solution is to use a computer stand.

Possible effect on fertility[edit]

A study by State University of New York researchers found that heat generated from laptops can increase the temperature of the lap of male users when balancing the computer on their lap, potentially putting sperm count at risk. The study, which included roughly two dozen men between the ages of 21 and 35, found that the sitting position required to balance a laptop can increase scrotum temperature by as much as 2.1 °C (4 °F). However, further research is needed to determine whether this directly affects male sterility.[64] A later 2010 study of 29 males published in Fertility and Sterility found that men who kept their laptops on their laps experienced scrotal hyperthermia (overheating) in which their scrotal temperatures increased by up to 2.0 °C (4 °F). The resulting heat increase, which could not be offset by a laptop cushion, may increase male infertility.[65][66][67][68][69]

A common practical solution to this problem is to place the laptop on a table or desk or to use a book or pillow between the body and the laptop.[citation needed] Another solution is to obtain a cooling unit for the laptop. These are usually USB powered and consist of a hard thin plastic case housing one, two, or three cooling fans – with the entire assembly designed to sit under the laptop in question – which results in the laptop remaining cool to the touch, and greatly reduces laptop heat buildup.

Thighs[edit]

Heat generated from using a laptop on the lap can also cause skin discoloration on the thighs known as "toasted skin syndrome".[70][71][72][73]

Durability[edit]

A clogged heat sink on a laptop after 2.5 years of use

Laptops are less durable than desktops/PCs. However, the durability of the laptop depends on the user if proper maintenance is done then the laptop can work longer.

Laptop keyboard with its keys (except the space bar) removed, revealing crumbs, pet hair, and other detritus to be cleaned away.

Equipment wear[edit]

Because of their portability, laptops are subject to more wear and physical damage than desktops. Components such as screen hinges, latches, power jacks, and power cords deteriorate gradually from ordinary use and may have to be replaced. A liquid spill onto the keyboard, a rather minor mishap with a desktop system (given that a basic keyboard costs about US$20), can damage the internals of a laptop and destroy the computer, result in a costly repair or entire replacement of laptops. One study found that a laptop is three times more likely to break during the first year of use than a desktop.[74] To maintain a laptop, it is recommended to clean it every three months for dirt, debris, dust, and food particles. Most cleaning kits consist of a lint-free or microfiber cloth for the LCD screen and keyboard, compressed air for getting dust out of the cooling fan, and a cleaning solution. Harsh chemicals such as bleach should not be used to clean a laptop, as they can damage it.[75]

Heating and cooling[edit]

Laptops rely on extremely compact

TWO

PERSONAL COMPUTER

As the personal computer (PC) became feasible in 1971, the idea of a portable personal computer soon followed. A "personal, portable information manipulator" was imagined by Alan Kay at Xerox PARC in 1968,[5] and described in his 1972 paper as the "Dynabook".[6] The IBM Special Computer APL Machine Portable (SCAMP) was demonstrated in 1973.[7] This prototype was based on the IBM PALM processor.[8] The IBM 5100, the first commercially available portable computer, appeared in September 1975, and was based on the SCAMP prototype.[9]

As 8-bit CPU machines became widely accepted, the number of portables increased rapidly. The first "laptop-sized notebook computer" was the Epson HX-20,[10][11] invented (patented) by Suwa Seikosha's Yukio Yokozawa in July 1980,[12] introduced at the COMDEX computer show in Las Vegas by Japanese company Seiko Epson in 1981,[13][11] and released in July 1982.[11][14] It had an LCD screen, a rechargeable battery, and a calculator-size printer, in a 1.6 kg (3.5 lb) chassis, the size of an A4 notebook.[11] It was described as a "laptop" and "notebook" computer in its patent.[12]

The portable micro computer Portal of the French company R2E Micral CCMC officially appeared in September 1980 at the Sicob show in Paris. It was a portable microcomputer designed and marketed by the studies and developments department of R2E Micral at the request of the company CCMC specializing in payroll and accounting. It was based on an Intel 8085 processor, 8-bit, clocked at 2 MHz. It was equipped with a central 64 KB RAM, a keyboard with 58 alphanumeric keys and 11 numeric keys (separate blocks), a 32-character screen, a floppy disk: capacity = 140,000 characters, of a thermal printer: speed = 28 characters / second, an asynchronous channel, asynchronous channel, a 220 V power supply. It weighed 12 kg and its dimensions were 45 × 45 × 15 cm. It provided total mobility. Its operating system was aptly named Prologue.

A Siemens PCD-3Psx laptop, released in 1989

The Osborne 1, released in 1981, was a luggable computer that used the Zilog Z80 and weighed 24.5 pounds (11.1 kg).[15] It had no battery, a 5 in (13 cm) cathode-ray tube (CRT) screen, and dual 5.25 in (13.3 cm) single-density floppy drives. Both Tandy/RadioShack and Hewlett Packard (HP) also produced portable computers of varying designs during this period.[16][17] The first laptops using the flip form factor appeared in the early 1980s. The Dulmont Magnum was released in Australia in 1981–82, but was not marketed internationally until 1984–85. The US$8,150 (equivalent to $22,880 in 2021) GRiD Compass 1101, released in 1982, was used at NASA and by the military, among others. The Sharp PC-5000,[18] Ampere[19] and Gavilan SC released in 1983. The Gavilan SC was described as a "laptop" by its manufacturer,[20] while the Ampere had a modern clamshell design.[19][21] The Toshiba T1100 won acceptance not only among PC experts but the mass market as a way to have PC portability.[22]

cooling systems involving a fan and heat sink that can fail from blockage caused by accumulated airborne dust and debris. Most laptops do not have any type of removable dust collection filter over the air intake for these cooling systems, resulting in a system that gradually conducts more heat and noise as the years pass. In some cases, the laptop starts to overheat even at idle load levels. This dust is usually stuck inside where the fan and heat sink meet, where it can not be removed by a casual cleaning and vacuuming. Most of the time, compressed air can dislodge the dust and debris but may not entirely remove it. After the device is turned on, the loose debris is reaccumulated into the cooling system by the fans. Complete disassembly is usually required to clean the laptop entirely. However, preventative maintenance such as regular cleaning of the heat sink via compressed air can prevent dust build-up on the heat sink. Many laptops are difficult to disassemble by the average user and contain components that are sensitive to electrostatic discharge (ESD).

Battery life[edit]

Battery life is limited because the capacity drops with time, eventually requiring replacement after as little as a year. A new battery typically stores enough energy to run the laptop for three to five hours, depending on usage, configuration, and power management settings. Yet, as it ages, the battery's energy storage will dissipate progressively until it lasts only a few minutes. The battery is often easily replaceable and a higher capacity model may be obtained for longer charging and discharging time. Some laptops (specifically ultrabooks) do not have the usual removable battery and have to be brought to the service center of their manufacturer or a third-party laptop service center to have their battery replaced. Replacement batteries can also be expensive.

Security and privacy[edit]

Main article: Laptop theft

Because they are valuable, commonly used, portable, and easy to hide in a backpack or other type of travel bag, laptops are often stolen. Every day, over 1,600 laptops go missing from U.S. airports.[76] The cost of stolen business or personal data, and of the resulting problems (identity theft, credit card fraud, breach of privacy), can be many times the value of the stolen laptop itself. Consequently, the physical protection of laptops and the safeguarding of data contained on them are both of great importance. Most laptops have a Kensington security slot, which can be used to tether them to a desk or other immovable object with a security cable and lock. In addition, modern operating systems and third-party software offer disk encryption functionality, which renders the data on the laptop's hard drive unreadable without a key or a passphrase. As of 2015, some laptops also have additional security elements added, including eye recognition software and fingerprint scanning components.[77]

Software such as LoJack for Laptops, Laptop Cop, and GadgetTrack have been engineered to help people locate and recover their stolen laptops in the event of theft. Setting one's laptop with a password on its firmware (protection against going to firmware setup or booting), internal HDD/SSD (protection against accessing it and loading an operating system on it afterward), and every user account of the operating system are additional security measures that a user should do.[78][79] Fewer than 5% of lost or stolen laptops are recovered by the companies that own them,[80] however, that number may decrease due to a variety of companies and software solutions specializing in laptop recovery. In the 2010s, the common availability of webcams on laptops raised privacy concerns. In Robbins v. Lower Merion School District (Eastern District of Pennsylvania 2010), school-issued laptops loaded with special software enabled staff from two high schools to take secret webcam shots of students at home, via their students' laptops.[81][82][83]

THREE

A LAPTOP

A laptop, laptop computer, or notebook computer is a small, portable personal computer (PC) with a screen and alphanumeric keyboard. Laptops typically have a clam shell form factor with the screen mounted on the inside of the upper lid and the keyboard on the inside of the lower lid, although 2-in-1 PCs with a detachable keyboard are often marketed as laptops or as having a laptop mode. Laptops are folded shut for transportation, and thus are suitable for mobile use.[1] Its name comes from lap, as it was deemed practical to be placed on a person's lap when being used. Today, laptops are used in a variety of settings, such as at work, in education, for playing games, web browsing, for personal multimedia, and for general home computer use.

As of 2021, in American English, the terms laptop computer and notebook computer are used interchangeably;[2] in other dialects of English, one or the other may be preferred. Although the terms notebook computers or notebooks originally referred to a specific size of laptop (originally smaller and lighter than mainstream laptops of the time),[3] the terms have come to mean the same thing and notebook no longer refers to any specific size.

Laptops combine all the input/output components and capabilities of a desktop computer, including the display screen, small speakers, a keyboard, data storage device, sometimes an optical disc drive, pointing devices (such as a touch pad or pointing stick), with an operating system, a processor and memory into a single unit. Most modern laptops feature integrated webcams and built-in microphones, while many also have touchscreens. Laptops can be powered either from an internal battery or by an external power supply from an AC adapter. Hardware specifications, such as the processor speed and memory capacity, significantly vary between different types, models and price points.

Design elements, form factor and construction can also vary significantly · between models depending on the intended use. Examples of specialized models of laptops include rugged notebooks for use in construction or military applications, as well as low production cost laptops such as those from the One Laptop per Child (OLPC) organization, which incorporate features like solar charging and semi-flexible components not found on most laptop computers. Portable computers, which later developed into modern laptops, were originally considered to be a small niche market, mostly for specialized field applications, such as in the military, for accountants, or traveling sales representatives. As portable computers evolved into modern laptops, they became widely used for a variety of purposes.[4]